Troll Magic

Troll Magic

HIDDEN FOLK FROM THE MOUNTAINS
AND FORESTS OF NORWAY

THEODOR KITTELSEN

TRANSLATED BY TIINA NUNNALLY

UNIVERSITY OF MINNESOTA PRESS

MINNEAPOLIS

LONDON

CONTENTS

Translator's Note   vii

TROLL MAGIC

The Forest Troll 3

On the Way to a Feast at the Troll Castle 7

The Fossegrim 11

The Dragon 15

Supernatural Creatures I 19

Supernatural Creatures II 23

The Nisse 27

The Hulder 33

The Mermaid 39

The Witch 43

On Mount Kolsaas 47

A Sea Troll 53

The Nøkk 57

The Draug 61

The Sea Serpent 69

The Troll Bird 73

A Jutul Battle 79

The Dying Mountain Troll 83

Chronology of the Life of Theodor Kittelsen   87

Title page to Theodor Kittelsen, *Troldskab*, 1892.

Translator's Note

Towering one-eyed trolls lumber through the forests, huge monsters with gaping jaws rise up from the sea, and shape-changing nøkk hide in the mountain lakes, eager to lure passersby to a watery death. These are some of the creatures that inhabit the art of Theodor Kittelsen. His world is both mysterious and familiar, sinister and humorous—a borderland between the human and the fantastical, rooted in Norway's majestic and untamed terrain. Kittelsen's visionary work made him one of Norway's most famous and popular artists during his lifetime. Today many of his paintings and drawings, especially of trolls, are immediately recognized as his art, even outside Scandinavia. Yet the remarkable books that he both wrote and illustrated are not as well known. Some of his writings, especially *Troldskab*, owe a great deal to traditional Norwegian legends and myths that were handed down for generations. The word "troldskab" refers both to the eerie, supernatural beings that were often the subject of these much-told tales and to the inexplicable acts of sorcery, conjuring, and trickery that seemed to plague so many people, even for an entire lifetime. Yet Kittelsen's stories and images are uniquely his own. This is the first English translation of *Troldskab*, now titled *Troll Magic*.

Theodor Kittelsen was born in 1857 in Kragerø, in the Telemark region of southern Norway. His relatively stable childhood was turned upside down when his father, a shopkeeper, died, leaving the family in poverty. Eleven-year-old Theodor's education came to an end, along with his dreams of any sort of artistic pursuits. To help support his family, he was apprenticed to a watchmaker, first in Kragerø and then in Arendal, Norway. But in 1870 a wealthy citizen, Diderik Maria Aall, discovered Theodor's talents and offered him the finances to move to Kristiania (now Oslo), where he studied drawing. Aall's patronage also allowed Theodor to spend four years at the art academy in Munich, from 1876 to 1880. That city had become a hub for many prominent Norwegian artists and authors, including Erik Werenskiold and Henrik Ibsen. It soon became clear, however, that genre painting, which focused on depicting domestic scenes of ordinary life, was not Kittelsen's forte. Nor was he particularly comfortable painting with oils. When Aall's support ended, Kittelsen struggled to keep going by selling drawings to German magazines, but eventually he had to return to Norway.

The fall of 1881 marked a turning point in Kittelsen's artistic development. On Werenskiold's recommendation he was hired by the renowned collector of Norwegian folktales, Peter Christen Asbjørnsen, to illustrate the book *Eventyrbog for Børn. Norske Folkeeventyr* (published in three volumes from 1883 to 1887). Over a period of nearly thirty years, Kittelsen created illustrations for subsequent editions of folktales collected and edited by Asbjørnsen and Moltke Moe, who was continuing the work of his father, Jørgen Moe. Through these illustrations, initially drawn with pen-and-ink or pencil, Kittelsen gradually found his personal style as an artist.

His emerging style also became evident in the many humorous illustrations that he later contributed to the anthology *Fra Alverdens gemytlige Lande*, issued in 1887 by the Danish publisher Ernst Bojesen. Kittelsen's drawings for this volume displayed many of the hallmarks of his art: a tendency toward caricature and exaggeration, an unrestrained imagination, and a satirical depiction of human society disguised in animal forms.

In the fall of 1882 Kittelsen received a stipend to travel to Paris but, unable to thrive in the city's artist milieu, he left after only eight months. He then began another prolonged stay in Munich, where he focused his attention on establishing himself as an illustrator. In spite of some success with drawings published in German magazines and newspapers, he experienced unrelenting financial woes that finally forced him to return to Norway permanently.

Then in 1887 he decided to accompany his sister and brother-in-law to Norway's northern archipelago of Lofoten, where he lived for more than a year. The dramatic natural setting, with its rugged mountain peaks, sheltered island bays, and abundant wildlife, inspired a surge of creative activity. Kittelsen completed a series of drawings and worked on "Ekko," one of his few attempts at a large oil painting. He also drew illustrations for Ibsen's play Peer Gynt and recorded his personal impressions of northern life and nature in the book Fra Lofoten.

The landscape also prompted Kittelsen to give visual form to many creatures of Norwegian myth and folklore. His visions of the sea draug, the nøkk, and the forest troll all appeared in his drawings, as well as in the stories that he now began to write. Five years later, in 1892, some of these stories and illustrations were published together as Troldskab.

While I was working on my translation of The Complete and Original Norwegian Folktales of Asbjørnsen and Moe, published by the University of Minnesota Press in 2019, I looked at dozens of Kittelsen's paintings and drawings. Some were included, along with Werenskiold's illustrations, in my Norwegian editions of the tales. I found more illustrations by Kittelsen online, and we eventually selected a few for the cover and interior of Norwegian Folktales. But I had never read any of Kittelsen's own texts. When I was asked to translate Troldskab, I assumed that his stories would be quite similar in style to the tales collected by Asbjørnsen and Moe. In fact, they turned out to be very different, and it was challenging to translate them into English.

Kittelsen's stories do not have the consistent, cohesive narrative voice that Asbjørnsen and Moe carefully developed for their collections. Nor do his stories make use of repetition to mimic the oral storytelling tradition. And in *Troldskab* there are no recurring, archetypal characters such as Ash Lad.

Instead, Kittelsen tells his stories with exuberance and whimsy, changing the stylistic approach to match whatever he was imagining and drawing. The stories range from a lyrical homage to the forest in the opening tale, to a humorous depiction of trolls walking in a circle for a hundred years, to a chilling encounter with the ominous draug.

Kittelsen's tales evince a great sense of immediacy. Sometimes he tells the story in the first person, as in "Supernatural Creatures II." Sometimes he addresses the reader directly with warnings and admonitions, as in the beginning of "The Nøkk." His stories are overflowing with vivid details and surprising events, both funny and scary.

Translating Kittelsen's tales brought me even closer to the astounding world he so clearly envisioned and portrayed in his art. These stories offer a delightful accompaniment to the formidable and compelling drawings that he chose for *Troldskab*.

Troll Magic

THE FOREST TROLL

The forest, the utter wildness of the forest, has left its mark on us. We've become part of its very nature. We love the forest exactly the way it is, strong and melancholy.

As children, we stared up into the gusty spruces and pines. We followed the mighty tree trunks with our eyes and our souls. We clambered among the strong, twisted arms to land in the very tops—in the swaying and gusting tops, up there in the lovely blue.

When the sun went down, loneliness and stillness spread across the sprawling heath, heavy and quiet. It was as if the heath didn't dare take a breath, as if the forest were waiting in motionless, hushed anticipation. Then our hearts began to pound. We wanted more. We begged and pleaded for adventures, strong and wild adventures for us poor children.

And the forest gave us adventures.

Huge and quiet, it came creeping, as if on soft, soundless cat paws.

Everything that had been frozen in place began to move.

Over there a rocky outcropping sprang up, gathering wonder and fear. It glanced around . . . began rising . . . then ambled in towering silence straight toward us! And we were gleeful with fright. We loved it!

That was the forest troll. In his single big eye he displayed all the eeriness and terror, all the gold and glittery sheen that our child-souls demanded.

We wanted to be scared—but we were also defiant! As small as we were, we wanted to tease him, charge at his heels, and steal his gold. But our greatest wish was to have that gleaming eye from his forehead. Who would have thought a hideous forest troll would possess such an eye!

That eye glinted and shone like broad daylight in the midst of dark night. What we previously walked past without a thought now looked wondrously bright in its glow. The forest stream rippled with a silvery luster and issued silvery clear notes. The spruce blossomed with reddening cones. And even the meager moss atop the rounded stone outcroppings swelled before us with such a wealth of color and splendor that, weeping, we threw ourselves at it as if to a mother's breast.

You deep and silent forest, we love you exactly the way you are. Strong and melancholy. You lovely children's picture book: the squirrel gnawing on a cone, the titmice up in the pine needles, the bear growling in the thicket. And then the forest troll comes trundling along with his head high above the treetops. "Hey! Hey, you!"

On the Way to a Feast at the Troll Castle

A feast was going to be held at the troll castle. But it was a long way there, so they decided to keep each other company and go together: Trond, Kaare, Ivar Eldførpungen, Baard, Bobben of Musgjerd, and old Guri Suppetryne.

They headed up slopes, they crossed ridges and the meandering, forested heights. The spruce and pine trees stood as dense as heather and were so tall that they reached all the way up to the trolls' waists. This caused the most trouble for Guri, who was lugging the sack of provisions on her back. But if they didn't arrive before a hundred years had passed, they still wouldn't be late, so they could take their time.

The tall dark mountains seemed to go on forever. The men cleared their throats and grumbled a bit, the children stared big-eyed, and Guri whined as she shambled along behind the others. But the troll men merely hitched up their trousers once in a while, and when the path was at its roughest they would grab hold of each other's tail and then resume trudging forward.

Finally they had walked so far that it was time to rest for a while. But when they were about to set off again, no one could agree on which way to go. Trond thought the right way was to follow his nose and proceed straight ahead. Ivar Eldførpungen swore it would be best to simply walk backward—and the more turned around the better. Then Guri began to wail and complain about the sack. Day by day it was getting heavier and heavier, while the provisions inside dwindled more and more. But she and everybody else had to keep going, so they set off along a path where other trolls had clearly walked before them. The path made a deep groove across all the mountain crests.

In a cluster of trees Bobben of Musgjerd stumbled, and when he fell one of his feet broke off. Ah, well, it could have been worse! They left the foot lying there and trudged on.

At long last they came to a place where they found another broken-off foot. And that was a great consolation for Bobben, because it's always good to know that you're not the only person to suffer misfortune here in the world. Nevertheless, they did think it strange.

After they had walked farther than far, they found another foot, and they thought that was even stranger. Bobben began to think the foot looked rather familiar.

"Trond!" he said.

"Yeah?" said Trond.

"I think that foot is mine!"

Then they realized that they had been walking in a circle for a hundred years. Kaare picked up the foot and flung it over the mountaintop. On the other side the foot plunged into a lake, and no doubt it's still there.

But Guri Suppetryne kept on complaining about the sack of provisions, which had rubbed a big hole in her back. She said that Ivar Eldførpungen should take a turn carrying the sack. But when they took it away from her, the old woman was so feeble that she lost her balance and landed on her head. They decided that the simplest thing to do was to give her the sack to carry again. Without it, her back seemed completely hollow and she couldn't stand up.

Finally they were heading along the right path. Far ahead in the distance, across the dark forested crests and beyond one deep blue ridge after another, something was flickering like a star. It trembled and quivered with a strange shimmer, first white, then golden, then blue or green. The old troll men nodded to each other. They were certain they could find the way there.

It was the troll castle.

The eyes of the troll children became bigger and bigger. They hadn't known there were so many magical things in the world. Oh my, oh my, how splendid! Just imagine: the castle was made of gold! Its image glinted and gleamed in the deep still water, and all around swam silver ducks, bobbing their heads. The trolls heard the swishing and humming of dancing and golden harps, and the tops of the dark pines rustled and sang. Inside the castle sat the fossegrim, playing his fiddle so fast that the strings flashed. The hulder was twirling so hard as she danced that her tail flew past the ears of the guests. Along the walls sat gigantic trolls and barrow-mound figures, drinking ale and mead from golden horns and big buckets. The nisser made a great ruckus as they performed a thousand pranks, dashing about and showing off their muscle. They fought and played tricks on each other, and they linked fingers with other nisser in tests of strength until their finger joints groaned.

Trudging over the big dark mountain crests came long processions of strange creatures. Some were so old that moss and small shrubs grew from them. Others were so ancient and bent with age that they looked like the twisted roots of pine trees and had to be carried. A great creaking and crashing and rattling could be heard, a gasping and a snuffling, for they all wanted to join in the celebration. They wanted to go inside the gold and glitter, inside the Soria Moria Castle that stood there, the troll castle shivering with lights and trembling with music.

THE FOSSEGRIM

Sit down at the top of a waterfall, preferably on a night when the moon shines bright. Then you'll both hear and see the fossegrim, the waterfall spirit.

Down below in the black cauldron, he's sitting inside the seething whirlpools of foam and playing the vast melodies of nature. At first there are only thunderous roars, but little by little the sounds seize hold of you, and you'll feel an urge to fling yourself down into the swirling tones.

Thundering here are all the songs that dwell in anxious stillness inside the forest and atop the mountains. All the voices of nature resonate from the strings of the fossegrim's fiddle. The dwarf's voice casts a circle around it all, making everything rise up as a mighty whole.

The spruce trees rustle, the aspens quiver, the streams ripple, and the birches tremble. From the mountain crests the fresh winds rejoice, the wooded silence sighs, and the quiet depths of the forest lake sing with the gentle, melancholy notes of the willow flute.

Dreaming, the fossegrim leans over his fiddle. With great resonant strokes the bow flits back and forth. Everything must be swept up in the notes, then sent outward to spill over the edge of the waterfall and into the whirlpool below!

The fossegrim plays the fiddle with his eyes closed, peering inside himself. He too is in the midst of all the swirling. Listen to the way he stomps his foot to keep time!

His playing is eternal. That's why the gleaming black mountain walls rise to a mighty temple where the sounds of eternity can freely roar. Sailing high above on the dark blue vault is the silvery clear moon, mirrored in the glittering serpentine coils of the deep black pools below.

Now star after star is lit overhead. The tones seem to grow wilder, as if every note wants to rise to the myriad stars and spread out to sparkle among them. But the fossegrim, that strong and wild fiddler, is sitting with his eyes closed, bending over his fiddle. His playing is the chain that binds him to the watery abyss.

THE DRAGON

For centuries the dragon brooded over the golden treasure, covering with its wings the royal crowns, the gemstones, and the chests filled with gleaming rings. The dragon kept guard with flashing eyes, and out of its maw poured fire and smoke. Occasionally it would amble out of its cave. The mighty, fearsome shape would rush across the sea, leaving traces of smoke and sparks in its wake. And people would fall to their knees to crawl into shadows and hiding places.

Few were those who dared venture to the dragon's cave to try and claim the glittering treasure. And no one ever returned. The sword might fly from its scabbard, but long before the blade struck the curving claws, the dragon's poisonous breath would eat right through any shield and kill the adversary. Bleached skulls lay all around, giving snakes and mice plenty of places to live.

But time conquered the terrifying dragon. It began to sleep longer and longer. Generations passed between each time the dragon flew out of its cave. With horror the new descendants would regard the dragon as an omen of wars and plagues and all things evil.

Now the omen has disappeared into slumber. The dragon has become a legend. It is sleeping the heavy sleep of death. Its eyes have sunk into its skull, its wings have grown stiff. The carved runes break apart, the death's-head crumbles, and time strews grass and moss over everything.

Rowan trees and bushes hide the cave. Out there everything is now so bright and sun-warmed. A gusting breeze rushes in from the churning sea, making the bushes and trees sway and rustle their leaves. And on a rowan branch a little bird perches, rocking back and forth.

"Cheep-cheep! I'm so happy, so happy! Down by the mountain wall I've built my nest of straw and mud. The sun shines into it, and the briar rose thicket has raised above it a flower to form a roof. Cheep-cheep!"

SUPERNATURAL CREATURES I

I once knew a young man who firmly believed in supernatural creatures. When I asked him whether he'd actually seen any, he replied, "No, I haven't, but my brother has. And my brother never lies."

The young man had been born on an island far out in the sea. Dilapidated hovels were scattered about, desolate and dreary and located far from each other. Rocks and stubbly mounds of grass were the only things in sight. The whole place was surrounded by open waters, encircling seaweed, and pale boulders over which the long sea swells poured.

His brother was a quiet and somber man. He said that when he lay awake during the bright summer nights he often heard hymns being sung outside, tunes that were so strangely gripping and enticing. One night as he lay in bed listening, it seemed as if creatures that he couldn't see were moving around him. Then a bustling and whispering started up, and all of a sudden the floor was covered with balls of gray woolen yarn leaping and springing about in a wild dance. The man sat up in bed. No sooner did he utter the name of Jesus than the balls of yarn swarmed toward the door of the stove and vanished in a puff of smoke. He heard them tumbling about inside the stove, and then everything grew quiet.

In the old days there were hordes of supernatural creatures everywhere. From hills and barrow mounds rang the sound of fiddles and folk tunes. Every once in a while a long bridal procession would pass by, a parade of tiny gray-clad men and women. They brought along golden horns and pitchers, and they invited their guests to drink. But woe to anyone who agreed to drink, for that person would then be in their power. As soon as dusk settled in, the old gray men would crawl out, and then it was dangerous to be outdoors, especially for young girls. Many a lovely girl has been lured by the supernatural creatures into the mountain and barrow mound, and there she has wandered about half-mad, muttering about her rich suitors, splendid livestock herd, and large estates.

Nor was it particularly pleasant to awaken in the middle of the night and see the room teeming with folks from the barrow mounds. All of them behaved as if they were in their own home, speaking in voices both loud and low. Greedy as they were, they would then seize all the good food they could find: sour-cream porridge and cured meat, rolled lefse and full-cream milk. They might even sniff around to find the dram bottle and the coarse-shredded tobacco. Scolding and cursing would do no good. It was best to fire a shot over the heads of those creatures. That got them going! Shouting and yelling, they would tumble out through all the holes and cracks like little gray balls of yarn.

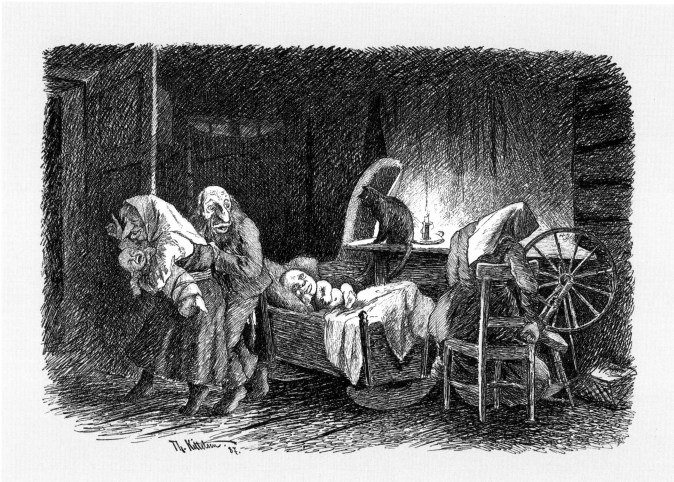

Supernatural Creatures II

It so happened that in bygone days the supernatural creatures often stole infants and then replaced them with young of their own. That sort of changeling was not a lovely sight: those creatures had a big head and few wits, and lay in the cradle all day long, doing nothing but wailing and crying.

I remember well one woman who was left to grapple with just such a changeling. She must have forgotten to put steel and a hymnal in the cradle with her newborn. The supernatural creatures came at once to whisk her child away. When the woman went to tend to her baby, she found a terribly ugly infant lying in the cradle. He had big, stupid eyes, and he was sucking on his finger. The woman was both dismayed and angry. She grabbed the changeling by the scruff of his neck and hauled him outside to the courtyard. There she whipped him so hard that he howled. But even though she whipped him on three Thursday nights in a row, the poor woman could not get rid of him.

When the changeling grew up he had a beard and was exceedingly loathsome in appearance. Talking was not something he could do. He barked like a fox and crawled around on all fours. In the daytime he sat outside on a stool next to the red-board wall of the house with a small green table in front of him. His plaything was a dinner knife. He would jab the blade into the crack of the table drawer and hit the knife so it said *whirr, whirr, whirr, whirr,* just like a spinning wheel. Once in a while he would stop abruptly and shout "Hans!" That was his name, and evidently it was the only word he could say. Then he would return to hitting the knife. Whirr, whirr, whirr, whirr!

But he was a sneaky fellow, all the same. Underneath the table he'd piled up a bunch of small stones. Whenever anyone happened to pass by, he was quick to slip his hand under the table . . . and zip! Out came a stone and flew at the person's head. Then the changeling would laugh so hard that the corners of his mouth stretched all the way to his ears.

THE NISSE

The nisse is a strange little goblin. He has only four fingers on each hand, for he has no thumbs. Yet it's probably best to stay on good terms with him. With those eight crooked little fingers of his, the nisse has seized many a mighty man and spun him around so that the man ended up crippled for the rest of his life. Otherwise the nisse is not so bad, as long as he gets his blessed porridge: that's something he has to have.

And porridge with a pat of butter is not really such an outlandish reward for all the work that the nisse does on the farm. He tends to the cows and takes care of the horses. He steals hay and grain from the large estate and toils the best he can for his own master. A farmstead without a nisse is not worth much.

But he certainly is a prankster. Everywhere, both up in the attic and in the barn, you can hear him chuckling and chortling and amusing himself. Most often he sits in the moonlight on the ramp leading to the barn and dangles his feet over the edge. He gets up once in a while to yank the cat's tail or tease the farm dog. Or he turns himself into a little lump and lies there as still as can be. If someone happens to come along and picks up the lump, wondering what it is ... *zip!* It flies out of the person's hand, and there stands the little, long-tailed nisse, roaring with laughter.

What the nisse likes best is spending time in the barn, where he rustles around in the hay, or in the dark attic among all the chests and old junk covered with dust and spiderwebs. The more cluttered it is up there, the more the nisse thrives. So many strange things can be found in an attic—rats and mice and fat spiders. The windowsill is littered with dead flies and long-legged mosquitoes. And if you happen to bump into the ragged sack hanging from a nail under the roofbeams, moths will come rushing out.

But at night it's not pleasant to lie in bed and listen to the nisse. Occasionally he tumbles around like a ball of yarn, and then he begins whistling and wheezing, and all of a sudden a terrific clatter starts up. Tin buckets topple on the floor, empty pots and bottles fall over, and hundreds of rat feet seem to be skittering around. Then everything abruptly goes quiet. And the nisse can keep this up all night long. Yet it's not so strange that most people have no desire to get out of bed and, wearing only a nightshirt, pad upstairs to the attic to see what's going on.

The fact that nighttime courting is also subject to the nisse's pranks is something that Olaves Lenæs, son of Berte Sutra, can confirm. Olaves was the nicest person ever to walk in two shoes—or rather, two sea boots, because he was a seaman, after all. Whenever he happened to get angry, he might wave his fist about, the way most folks do, in order to emphasize what he was saying. But he wouldn't pound his fist on the table like the others; he was much too well bred for that. No, Olaves would merely raise his fist and scowl at the table. Then he would lean down and slam his fist on the floor with such force that it sang.

When he was courting Olava, he would often arrive a bit late in the evening to visit her. One night he noticed that everyone had already gone to bed and everything was quiet. He had to make his way through the brew house, but he thought it would be a disgrace and a shame to disturb anyone. So Olaves took off his boots and set them behind a garbage pail full of fish guts and other trash. Cautiously, in his stocking feet, he padded his way upstairs to visit his sweetheart. When he came back down, his boots were gone. He was positive that he'd left them behind the garbage pail, yet now they weren't there.

What the devil! thought Olaves. He fumbled around in the dark, trying to find them. All of a sudden he stumbled over his boots, and then he clearly heard a snickering and snorting from a corner of the room. Good thing I found my boots, thought Olaves. But strangely enough they were as heavy as lead. When he had a good look at them, he saw that they were stuffed with all sorts of waste from the garbage pail. Olaves was so enraged that he flung the boots at the wall, making fish guts and mackerel milt spray everywhere. The nisse found it all very entertaining! Over in the corner he laughed and hooted as if he might burst.

The nisse certainly caused a lot of havoc at that particular house. It was one of those old white-painted timber buildings with a steep stairway in front. The house stood there with a great air of conceit, peering at the neighbor houses out of the corner of its eye. The homeowner was an organist, a dry old geezer with a black stain under his nose from snuff. The strangest thing about him was his chin, which jutted out so far that below his mouth his jaw looked exactly like a cream pitcher. Every time I looked at that pitcher-face of his, he would smile and greet me with such sneering arrogance that I always regretted being the first to doff my hat and step forward. His sister, who kept house for him, was an old spinster. Around her neck she wore on a string a heart-shaped silver locket, which she constantly opened and sniffed. She was the one who had the most to do with the nisse.

In that house it was apparently quite difficult for the nisse to get any porridge, and that's why he created as much commotion as he could: it was his means of revenge. At night he would make such a racket that it was impossible for anyone to sleep. Downstairs in the kitchen the plates and platters would fall off the shelves on the wall, while smoke and sparks flew out of the stove. Then all the windows and doors had to be opened. And the windowpanes were splattered with paper spitballs that made the glass crack in every direction. Yet things got even worse in the winter. That's when the nisse would throw open the attic windows and let the snow blow inside to settle on the floor in big drifts. Though the food might have been scanty, the nisse certainly couldn't complain about a lack of amusements at the organist's house!

The neighbors claimed that one night they had actually seen the nisse dancing around the stairs with the housekeeper's gray cat. The cat was hissing and making a fuss worse than sin, because the nisse had grabbed both of its forepaws and was swinging the cat around as he trilled:

You and me and that old shrew,
You and me and that old shrew,
For crusted porridge we fight and feud!

Ah, yes, the old spinster with the heart-shaped silver locket might well have had a few tales to tell about that nisse if only she were willing to talk. But her brother, being the aristocrat that he was, would always smile arrogantly whenever such topics happened to come up. Out of his cream-pitcher jaw these words would inevitably issue: "Yes indeed, my sister and those nisse stories of hers! My sister is such a big fool."

THE HULDER

When the hulder plays the zither called a *langeleik*, she doesn't sit there brooding over the tune. Her eyes whirl in her skull as she peers and stares all around. She's looking to see if some fine lad might show up, someone with whom she could have a bit of fun. She is a fine gal, if only she didn't have that ugly cow tail. But usually she makes sure to hide her tail so it's impossible to tell that she's any different from other women.

Jens Kleiva had convinced himself that he was a handsome man—yes, he certainly had. He believed that all womenfolk would go crazy for him the minute they set eyes on him. And he swore not to give up until every girl in the whole countryside had fallen unhappily in love with him. He was sure this had already happened to at least six girls so far.

"The seventh is bound to be Margit Braaten," he murmured to himself. He happened to be sitting in his shirtsleeves as he whittled a big flute of willow.

"Hey!" a voice suddenly shouted in his ear.

Jens gave a start. In front of him stood a girl of such dazzling beauty that he'd never in his life seen anything like it.

"What are you whittling, Jens?" she asked.

"Oh, it's just a willow flute," he said. "I wanted to see if it might be possible to play some sort of melody."

"Give it a try, Jens! For you, I'm sure that would be no problem at all."

Jens wanted to please her. But what the devil! The lovely girl sat there, staring and staring at him so intently that his face turned bright red. And he couldn't seem to make his mouth work properly. No matter how he pursed his lips and blew into the flute, the only sounds that came out were pt . . . pt-ut . . . pt-petu!

"Ah, well," she said. "Not everyone is cut out for greatness. But let me give it a try."

I have to tell you that such joyous sounds then issued from the willow flute. And Jens turned as tender as a rolled lefse. When the lovely girl played that flute, both the flute and Jens wept.

And with that, he felt an urge to woo her. "Oh, would you . . . would you be my sweetheart?" he asked.

That might not be such a bad idea, she told him.

I knew this would happen, thought Jens.

But she proposed three conditions. If he could meet these terms, she would be his, along with the farmstead and land that she owned. First, he must not ask for her name until their wedding day. Second, he must wait until that day to mention to a single living soul what had just happened. Third, he would have to wait a year until they could meet again.

"Fine," said Jens. "I agree to all of that."

Then she took out something and smeared it on the willow flute. "If you're fond of me, you'll bring this flute with you the next time we meet," she said.

Yes, she could count on him for that, Jens told her.

No sooner had she left than Jens dashed from one farm to the next, boasting and bragging in the worst way. He couldn't resist telling everyone that he was now betrothed. And with a stupendously rich girl who owned a farm and land and big forests and hundreds of cattle. In the surrounding countryside there wasn't a single girl who suited him enough that he would bother to stand up in her presence, even if he was doing nothing but sitting on his backside atop a pile of hemp. So those girls were all welcome to stay right where they were!

He grew so smug that he spent every day idly wandering about with his fists stuffed in his pockets. Lord Jens was devising and planning his wedding, for he wanted it to be acclaimed far and wide. Six musicians would walk at the front of the procession, two playing drums and four playing fiddles. Four stout men wearing top hats would brandish pistols and fire shots the whole way. And six footmen would dash around, pouring ale and liquor for every mouth. Then Jens and his bride would appear, riding splendid horses and wearing gilded silver crowns on their heads. And following them would come an endless entourage, because everyone was invited, the whole countryside, both the lowly and the rich.

The other promises Jens did keep. A year later, to the day, he took his willow flute and sat down in the same place where he'd met the beautiful girl. He decided to play a tune.

But the flute seemed to have dried up. Ugh, how awful it sounded! How it screeched and scratched! Not a single note came out,

not even *pt-tu*, *pt-tu*. The only sound was a hoarse squeaking of words: "Big braggart Jens! Numbskull Jens! Pack-of-lies Jens! Stupid Jens!"

"Hey!" shouted someone in his ear. And there stood the girl, her eyes shining. She reached back to grab fistfuls of her flaxen hair and held the tresses out to either side, where they gleamed in the sun.

"I suppose now I can ask you what your name is," said Jens.

"I'm called Hulder," she said. "But I have to tell you, Jens, that a slovenly person like you is not someone I would ever want to have, even if you threw yourself at me. You're just like that dried-up flute of yours—yes, you are!"

"Now, wait a minute," said Jens. "You won't get away with that! For every finger on my hands I could count at least twelve girls who are your equal. Though I suppose not one of them has a tail."

"But I do. And now you're going to get a taste of it!" shouted the hulder.

Then she grabbed hold of her cow tail with both hands and whipped it at Jens's ears so hard that he collapsed in a faint.

He suffered the effects of that ear-boxing for the rest of his life. Hard of hearing and dim-witted, he wandered from farm to farm and from village to village, carrying a sack. But his fondness for girls stayed with him to the end. Whenever the poor fool arrived at a farm, someone would always ask him, "I suppose there are plenty of splendid girls back in your village, Jens. Am I right?"

Then his whole face would light up. "Oh, yes, they're certainly splendid and fine, that they are!"

THE MERMAID

Surely you know the dreaming bird
that floats and dozes on waves of foam.
Where is its home? Where is the shelter
that it seeks in its dreams?

—Johan Welhaven

The sea is lovely when, gleaming and still, it sways with gentle, rolling waves. Whispering all around and far into the distance is a dreamlike rushing sound, a trembling and melancholy yearning. But loveliest of all is when the sea and air merge into one, and the noisy world lies far, far away in outlines of surging blue.

Then the mermaid rises from the deep. Her long golden hair floats around her, and with wet, sea-deep eyes she casts a dreaming gaze at the blue shoreline. Beads of foam bubble and spill around her. Yet she merely stares and stares, as if her thoughts were sailing on white wings far away in the hidden realm of eternity.

What could she be dreaming about?

No, don't try to catch the buoyant-winged gull! Instead watch how the bird playfully dances on its slender wings, how it soars and sinks!

Over there beyond the blue-tinged shores the tumultuous world resounds. Did it give to you the gold of your dreams? Did your own thoughts fly like birds in restless pursuit, though you had no idea where they were headed?

From the fathomless deep she brings forth tones—a muted, hidden song. Down below among the seaweed and corals and teeming, crawling creatures—that's where her sense of longing grew. She needed to rise above the confining surface, up into the light to take a look at the vaulting sky.

Hush! Listen to her singing.

Her voice resonates with the lovely purity of a child. All around her the tones ripple and flow into each other like sea foam, quivering between tears and joy. The seabird pauses to listen. It understands her so well. Then the bird plucks a feather to adorn its poor breast, restlessly lifts its wings, and quick as lightning dives into the deep.

The sun is sinking lower and lower. The sea and the sky are swathed in a golden light. The mermaid is still singing her lovely songs. Then the disk of the sun dips into the sea, and the tones quaver with melancholy. One more trembling second . . . and then the sun sets and the mermaid is gone.

Oh, how cold it is! The sea is now dark and churning. The winds race across the surface, plowing up the water into leaping, foaming swells. Out on the black skerries, a seal crawls out of the kelp to lie there and stare with icy sorrow across the dismal blue-blackness. A schooner appears, its sails full and billowing. The ship cuts and cleaves through the sea, making the foam crash around her bow. They're sailing for both their livelihood and their fortune, for cargo and gold. "Hey, boys! Time to reef the sails! Night is coming, and we're in for a storm."

THE WITCH

The fact that Old Erik, who so shamelessly runs about on land and shore, manages to wear out both his shoes and his socks is something that anyone might easily understand.

Yet he too has his devoted attendants. Take a look at the old witch up there on the mountain ledge. She works for Old Erik, and you'd have to look long and hard to find a more diligent creature. The wages aren't especially good, but they're satisfactory. Last time he paid her for a pair of knitted stockings by tickling her under the arm. "Tickle, tickle, tickle!" He kept doing that until the calves of her legs began to cramp. And that was payment enough, in my view.

"Oh, yes, socks he shall have—good, warm socks for Old Erik, that poor man."

Things have not gone well for Old Erik lately, and few people have any desire even to acknowledge they know him. The only ones willing to do so are those he likes the least. Now he runs around with his tongue hanging out in an attempt to sell two or three paltry items, junk that could just as well be sold off at a public auction along with other trash. Practically everywhere he goes these days, at every door he knocks, he ends up being sent away with the same sort of rude greeting: "I don't know you, my man. So excuse me. Goodbye!"

"Oh, yes, stockings he shall have—stockings for Old Erik, that poor man. He honestly and justly deserves them."

Whirr, whirr, whirr, whirr, whirr.

Didn't Old Erik get a pair of socks as a Christmas present last year? Yes, my goodness, he most certainly did. But he wore out those socks until they were a pitiful sight. And wasn't that to be expected? Slovenly man that he is, he trudged around through thick and thin, in both hot and cold weather, never bothering to change his socks even once. Finally only the knitted cuffs and ankles were left. But the old man merely pulled them down over his toes and tied the opening closed with a piece of twine. And he kept wearing those socks that way as he ran around until they finally fell off in tatters.

But you should know that the wool used for Old Erik's socks is not of ordinary quality. Otherwise the socks certainly wouldn't last long at all. The wool for the yarn does look quite strange, both shaggy and finely carded, as it lies there in the witch's basket. The wool has been blended with stupidity and backbiting, gossip, envy, malice, and devilment. But more than half has been formed of stupidity, because stupidity gives the yarn such a light gray color. And it makes the loveliest, softest socks that anyone could ever wish to wear.

But socks are not the only things the witch, that woman who sits up there on the mountain ledge, needs to make for Old Erik. Next to her wool basket is a pile of the most splendid raw material used for evil and venom. And it all has to be finished in good time. So it's best if she gets to work now, the spinning wheel moving fast enough to make sparks fly!

ON MOUNT KOLSAAS

Miss Enersen, who happened to be visiting Madam Syvertsen, was weeping over all the sin and evil in the world. She wept tears as big as coffee beans, and her nose wept, too, so that her checked handkerchief had to keep rising, eager to be of service.

Who the devil would ever believe that Miss Enersen was a witch! Yet only a few hours later she was back home, greasing her birch-twig broom.

Up on Mount Kolsaas a big meeting of witches was going to take place. The Devil himself had promised to make an appearance and bring along his fiddle. So this time it was important to make a special effort in what she wore. That's why all the dresser drawers stood open in Miss Enersen's house. And scattered around were pieces of lace, pantalettes, bottles of scent, petticoats, wiglets, and all sorts of other frippery. At long last she was ready.

Then she climbed astride her broom. "Upside-down and downside-up, off to Kolsaas!" she said. And up through the chimney the broom flew, making soot swirl around her.

It so happened that Anne, the kitchen maid, was standing behind the closed door. And through the keyhole she saw every little detail.

At first Anne couldn't understand why Miss Enersen was putting on her finery so late at night. But then she saw her mistress take out of the dresser a billy-goat horn and smear something from it on her broom. That's when

Anne understood the reason for it all. And she had a great urge to go along. She thought to herself: Surely it can't be that dangerous, just this once. She never had much fun in that house, where her time was spent endlessly laboring with the pots and dishrags.

So she opened a drawer of Miss Enersen's dresser and liberally smeared the back of it with the same salve.

I need to make sure I come back a little earlier than the mistress, thought Anne. Then she won't notice a thing.

Going up the chimney was a tight fit, but once she was outside in the air, it turned out that she'd made quite a good choice of transport. Outdoors there was plenty of room for the drawer in which she sat. She flew upside down so that it seemed to her the whole world was falling out of the dresser drawer and into a deep black hole below. The clouds were made of the finest wool, and the moon tumbled from one cloud to the next, bright and polished shiny. Oh, she had such an urge to reach out her finger to touch the moon! But that would have to wait for another time. Onward she flew, with the clouds surging around the dresser drawer.

Suddenly she began to sink and sink. The clouds hung like woolen rags around her. Bam! There she lay on Mount Kolsaas with her arms and legs sticking up in the air and a big crack in the bottom of the drawer.

On a ridge some distance away glowed a huge bonfire. It was important to be cautious. Anne picked up three big rocks and set them in the drawer. On top she placed two sticks so they formed a cross. Then she crept as close to the bonfire as seemed sensible and hid inside a mountainside crevice.

Around the bonfire sat a big group of witches. Some were knitting stockings and some were crocheting trim.

Maybe you think they were crocheting lace? Oh, yes, such lovely lacework! The top edges looked nice enough, but at the bottom every piece of lace ended in a big tangle of hissing snake-heads. Nor would you take much pleasure from the stockings they were knitting. The top part was wearable enough, but each stocking ended in a big pouch stuffed full of poisons and venom.

A great babbling issued from the witches. All of them were laughing and talking at once, mocking and scolding, gossiping and cackling so loud that it was loathsome to hear.

Anne sat nestled inside the crevice, thinking it was such great fun. She began to look around to see if there was anyone she recognized.

Well, there was Miss Enersen, but of course she already knew her mistress was present. And the pharmacist's wife—just imagine, the pharmacist's wife! And was that actually Miss Adriansen over there? And Katrine Bøllom? And Severine Trap as well! Malla Børresen with her toothache was there, too. What the devil! Good gracious, there sat old Berte Haugane, who sold blueberries and smelled like a cowshed. And she was sitting there so amiably next to that haughty Miss Ulrikka Prebensen. How astonishing to see her beside that snooty

woman who always said to the grocer, "Be so good as to serve me first!"

Anne had to bite her thumb to keep from laughing.

Words flew out of everyone's mouth like yarn from a spinning wheel. Right now they were ranting on and on about the pastor's wife—that little bookworm who clung so tightly to that fat pulpit of a man. She really ought to watch her step. Yes, she should! Then the talk switched to the county governor's wife, the judge's wife, the sheriff's wife, and many more.

Everybody was speaking at such a furious pace that their jaws ended up juddering with Saint Vitus's dance.

Then Miss Enersen shouted, "We spit on them all! Ptui!"

"Ptui! Ptui! Ptui!" everyone chimed in.

"I'm spitting too! Yes, I am!" said Berte Haugane. And they all laughed.

At that moment a vile black raven appeared. "He's on his way! He's on his way!" cried the bird.

The next second a tall, black vagabond arrived with a great deal of flapping and landed in their midst. Under his arm he carried a fiddle.

"Good evening, my friends!" he said.

"Welcome, welcome, dear Satan!" they replied. And then began a merriment and rejoicing beyond all measure. Finally they gathered their wits enough to remember the coffee pot they had put on the fire for the Devil. And what coffee it was! So strong and hot that everybody got as wobbly as knaves. The Devil, however, was no doubt used to such strong brew, for he swallowed a fistful of glowing embers with every cup he drank.

All of a sudden the Devil leaped into the middle of the bonfire and began playing the witches' dance so that flames shot out from the strings of his fiddle. All the witches grabbed each other by the hand and danced in a circle around him.

Anne had never heard or seen anything so vile.

It sounded as if someone were scratching a stone against a glass windowpane. And there was nothing in the whole world as nasty as that ugly creature with horns sprouting from his forehead who now stood in the middle of the fire!

How those witches leaped and carried on! The dance got wilder and wilder. Everyone whirled and spun like mad. Yet as eerie as the scene looked, Anne was so convulsed with laughter that she had to bite her thumb again. Oh, yes, gracious me! You should have seen Miss Prebensen, with her nose in the air, her silk gown rustling around those dried-out shins of hers, and with a delighted smile tugging at the corners of her mouth. Next to her was Berte Haugane, jumping and leaping and shouting, "Hopsa, hoopla!"

And even the sight of Miss Enersen . . . ha, ha, ha!

But most amusing of all was when Malla Børresen toppled over in the middle of the dance, and her long nose broke right off. Then everyone bellowed with laughter. Even the vile vagabond who sat in the midst of the flames roared.

But Anne was a sly girl.

It's best to leave some fun for another time, she thought.

Quietly she crept back to the dresser drawer. She took out the rocks and climbed in. "Upside-down and downside-up, away from Kolsaas!" she cried. And with great speed, the drawer carried her back home.

The next day Miss Enersen stood at her dresser and wondered why one of the drawers had a big crack in the bottom.

And Malla Børresen? She must have fallen down the stairs, for she had a big bandage on her nose.

When Anne went over to the grocer to buy two kinds of green soap, there was no getting around it—she had to bite her thumb yet again. Because in sailed that well-mannered lady with her nose in the air and her silk gown rustling around her dried-out shins. "I would like three *skillinger* worth of crimped hairpins," she said. "And be so good as to serve me first!"

A Sea Troll

Johan Persa and Elias Nilsa once went out to the islets together to shoot seabirds and gather eggs. Their efforts were rewarded. They collected a whole crate of eggs and also nabbed quite a few fat common eiders. They'd brought along a coffee pot and some provisions, and in the stern of their rowboat lay a little flask that was meant to lift their spirits. They made a fire, smoked their tobacco, and chatted a bit about the troubles of the world.

"All right, you can stay here and mind the coffee pot, Johan. I'm going out to fish for a while," said Elias.

Elias got one nibble after another, but not even a haddock did he catch. Yet it was strange about all those nibbles. He definitely had the feeling that something like a fist was tugging on his line, even though he pulled up an empty hook each time. He began to sense that something out of the ordinary must be nibbling at his line down below.

Elias wasn't stupid. He chuckled to himself and thought: If you're that hungry, then have a taste of this. He picked up an old furry mitten, filled it with dirt and debris, and attached it to his hook.

And with that he got a strong nibble. He pulled as hard as he could, but it was as if the line were tied to the bottom. Suddenly it released. He felt something heavy hanging on to it, and he heaved and heaved. Then the line got stuck again, and he couldn't budge it at all.

But Elias refused to give up. He merely coiled the line around an oarlock, spat on his hands, and then pulled with all his might. Suddenly the line was moving easier—so easy that he thought the hook must have fallen off. But as soon as the fishing sinker rose above the surface, he saw a big scorpion fish wriggling back and forth with the furry mitten in its jaws. The next second the fish fell to the bottom of the boat with a thud. There it lay, staring up at Elias.

Never had he seen anything so vile. The mouth was wide open with the hook and the mitten hanging from one corner. The fish was gasping and groaning, making its whole body rise and fall like a big bladder, while its tiny angled eyes spun around in its head. The fish was covered all over with barbs and little flaps of skin that wobbled and swayed.

Elias found it annoying that the fish had fooled him so badly. "Go ahead and stare, old man!" he said. "But I'll be damned if I'm afraid of you!" Then he grabbed the fish, yanked out the hook, and spat his whole wad of snuff right into its mouth. "You filthy beast!" he said, and then he angrily hurled the fish far across the water.

One day a long time after that, Elias happened to go to the same skerry to fish. This time he was alone. He moored his boat in a spot that was sheltered from the waves and settled down in the same place as before to make coffee. While the coffee brewed, he wandered around the islet. He looked at the black guillemots calling shrilly as they perched in crevices and hollows with the sea swirling around them. Then he happened to think about that vile scorpion fish he'd caught in this very place. At that moment he looked down, and he couldn't believe his eyes. There lay that same ugly beast on dry ground!

Well, the otter must have dragged it there, because that fish couldn't possibly be alive. And it did look dry as dust. Elias poked at the fish a bit with his foot. It turned out there was life in that fish after all! It jumped and leaped and snapped its jaws like crazy.

Then Elias gave the fish a mighty kick, and it flew at once into the sea.

But no sooner did the fish touch the water than it grew and grew into a horribly ugly fellow that rose up and gaped with scorpion fish jaws that were as huge as an open sea chest. And then he roared:

"Go ahead and spit into my mouth again, if you like, Elias! But let me tell you that I—"

Not another word did Elias hear. He ran as if the Devil himself were at his heels. He sped home, using both oars and sail, and with sweat pouring off him. Only when he had safely reached home did he remember the coffee pot that was still out there, boiling away.

THE NØKK

The nøkk is a cunning creature. He's on the hunt for human lives. When the sun sets, you'd better watch out.

He might be lying inside that big, glorious water lily that you're reaching for. No sooner do you touch the lily than the quagmire sinks beneath you, and the nøkk grabs you with his slimy wet hands.

Or when you're sitting all alone by the mountain tarn one evening, memories may appear, one after another, until they're soon swarming all around. Memories with the same warm color and sheen as the rays of light mirrored between the leaves and water lilies. But watch out! Those are strings upon which the nøkk is playing. The tarn conjures forth memories while the nøkk lies below, biding his time. He knows that he can easily catch us in that lovely, trembling mirrored image.

The nøkk can transform himself into every possible shape. He often lies on the shore as a piece of jewelry, glittering strangely. If you touch it, you'll be in his power. So sly is the nøkk that he can even stretch out in the grass as a forgotten fishing pole, complete with line and hook.

He has another favorite trick, but he has used it so often that hardly anyone falls for it anymore. He changes himself into an old flat-bottomed rowboat that has been pulled partway up on shore. Occasionally some fool does happen along, and when he sees the rowboat, this is what he thinks: Oh, what an old scow that is! And it's half-full of water. But I do believe I see an old tin bucket! And then he starts bailing out the boat, which is actually the nøkk. After that, the fellow shoves the boat into the water and climbs in.

At first everything is fine, because the nøkk wants to play with his prey, the way a cat toys with a mouse. Oh, how lovely it is to glide among the water lilies. The lake is so sparkling and still that every dip of the oars seems a sinful disturbance. Off in the distance floats a little island with a lone birch tree. How fun it would be to go there!

But in the middle of the lake the old rowboat starts leaking and leaking. Then cracks appear, and the boat sinks more and more. And with that the nøkk wraps himself around his prey and drags him down into the deep.

Sometimes the nøkk turns himself into a dapple gray horse grazing right next to the mountain tarn. He wants to lure somebody onto his back, and then he'll carry him straight down into the water.

There once was a farmer who caught sight of that gray horse. The animal was so fat that his coat gleamed, and the farmer thought it was an exceedingly splendid work horse. But he scratched his head as he pondered where that horse might have come from. He really couldn't understand it. Finally he went back home to get a halter, which he hid under his coat. When he returned, the work horse was still there, chomping and gnawing on grass.

"All right, my good colt! Come here, colt, come here!" said the farmer.

And the horse came. Yes, he did. The nøkk's only thought was to get this farmer's old carcass up on his back.

At that instant the farmer stuck his fists into both nostrils of the horse, and with that a wild dancing started. No matter how the horse strained and kicked, it did no good. In a flash the halter was slipped over the animal's head. Then the farmer gave the horse a friendly slap on his gleaming fat flank. "Now you'll have to come with me, my boy!" he said.

Then the nøkk was in the farmer's power. But the work horse was not a gentle beast when he was locked inside the stifling stable. The nøkk was used to lying in the fresh water of the tarn and peering out from the water lilies. And things weren't much better when the horse was allowed outside. That's when the farmer used the animal to plow his fields. The horse pulled the plow so hard that the earth flew all around, for he had the strength of at least twenty horses.

This horse is worth his weight in gold, thought the farmer. He works like the Devil himself, and he eats nothing.

But occasionally the man would flinch when he saw the animal's wild eyes glaring at him with such a strange, watery-green gaze. And when the sun went down, the gray horse would turn so wild and frenzied that it was unwise for any living thing to stay inside the stable. The horse whinnied and screeched all night, straining and pawing at the ground so that wood chips swirled through the stall.

At first the farmer found all of this quite amusing. But little by little he began to feel strangely burdened. He could never find any peace. A tight band seemed to be pressing around his head, and all he could do was utter a few croaks. He kept imagining that he saw streaks and stripes mirrored in deep, dark water, and that he was sinking and sinking into a bottomless mire.

"I'll give you ten *daler* if you'll take the halter off the gray horse, Ola!" he said to his servant boy.

"Ha! I'll do it for twelve *skillinger*," said Ola.

But when the halter was removed from the gray horse, it was too late. The animal slammed straight through the stable wall, smashing the broken timbers to either side.

Old Inger Bakken, who lived by the tarn, reported that the dapple gray work horse came racing at full gallop across her potato fields. "Smoke was pouring out of his nostrils, and his tail stood straight up like a billy-goat horn," she said. "And how he flew! Bless me if he didn't plunge right into the water so the foam rose up all around him like a rail fence!"

THE DRAUG

Kristian Westerval lived at a distant fishing station right next to the sea. He's dead and gone now, but many might still remember him.

He ran a mercantile shop out there and was considered a prosperous man, but also an odd character whom no one ever fully understood. There was always something melancholy and sorrowful about him. He was powerfully built with scant, snow-white hair and pale, impassive features. He was as gentle and soft-hearted as a child but also as stubborn as a goat, when it came right down to it.

Westerval was known to be an unusually skillful skipper at sea. But twice he'd ended up in the drink under a capsized boat and,

according to rumor, it had been foretold that the third time he wouldn't get out. So it was a good thing that he'd grown quite cautious of late; he almost never got into a boat anymore.

The house where he lived was one of the strangest places imaginable. To ease the coming and going of the fishermen, one side of the house was built into the mountain, while the other stood on pilings right over the water. A number of stairways and ladders led from the openings in the floor down to the sea. That's where fishermen could always be found as they busied themselves with their boats. The dock was built next to the house, extending along the mountainside, and it was always lined with scores of fish that had been hung up to dry. Here too you had to climb up through a rectangular opening while your boat was tied to the ladder underneath the planks of the dock.

Inside the main building there was a warehouse with multiple doors and hoist mechanisms. There were barrels filled with goods, sacks of flour, ropes, casks of tar, and dried fish stacked in great heaps. Barrels of eiderdown stood everywhere, and on the walls hung hundreds of razorbills, puffins, seagulls, and terns. Over in a corner otter and cormorant skins had been nailed to the wall, soft side out.

Westerval carried on a lively bartering trade with the fishermen, and nearly all of them had ended up in his pocket. They brought him everything—conches, corals, strange types of fish and starfish—and in return they received coffee and coarse-shredded tobacco.

Westerval lived alone in the house with his housekeeper. Most likely she found it quite dreary and unpleasant out there, but he did not. He loved the sea and the solitude.

His bedroom was the strangest thing of all in that strange house. He rarely slept more than a couple of hours, and never until well into the morning. He said that so many burdensome thoughts would occur to him that he could find no peace at night. Above the headboard of his bed he'd nailed a shelf for his lamp, and he would read novels all night long. Covering the walls was old wallpaper that sagged with big folds and bulges. And inside those slumped spaces rats would tumble and squeak, giving Westerval plenty of entertainment at night. He said that sometimes the rats would make such a ruckus that the folds in the wallpaper would rise and sink like ocean waves. The small room was filled with all manner of things. The table and windowsill were littered with tobacco, pipes, pipe cleaners, empty bottles, rocks from which coral grew, and all sorts of other items. Fastened to the wall was a heavy bookcase crammed with old books. Scattered about were crates and chairs. In one corner was an old sofa with the horsehair stuffing peeking out. And right next to the sofa hung six or seven pendulum clocks, both big and small, that kept up a terrible racket. Westerval thought the clocks were good company.

One night Westerval lay in bed puffing on his pipe. He was in the middle of an interesting chapter in an old novel. Outside a ferocious storm was roaring and making the old weathervane on the roof spin like a windmill as it screeched and scraped. The house creaked, the wind whistled through all the cracks, and the old wallpaper bulged in the shifting air pressure.

All of a sudden there was a mighty slap on the floor right under the bed. It sounded as if someone had struck the underside of the floorboards with a big wet mitten. The window rattled for so long afterward that it was quite spooky. Westerval was a brave man, but that didn't stop him from turning a bit paler than usual. Below he heard the sea surging with great slurping sounds. There was a rushing among the rocks down there, and at brief intervals a loud crashing sound would come from the mountain wall. As day neared, Westerval slept his regulation hours. In the morning he clambered down through the hatch in the floor. Below, the sea was still in a violent uproar, with the waves noisily leaping and foaming. A huge pile of seaweed had collected under the floor. Otherwise there was nothing out of the ordinary to be seen.

That fierce storm was not about to let up. Day by day it got worse. But since it was so late in the fall, that was only to be expected. One pitch-dark evening, Westerval was alone in his shop, having locked the door after a hectic day. Fishermen had crowded into the shop, and traces of their sea boots were still visible on the wet, muddy floor. Westerval was busy with the cash drawer, counting the money and adding amounts on a piece of wax paper with a pencil. Then he began cutting up the loose tobacco into small pieces for the following day before going over to the shelves to straighten up a bit.

"Well, well! In God's name, I'm glad this day is finally over," he said.

Then somebody suddenly appeared in the shop over by the door. In the light from his candle stump, Westerval saw a gigantic fellow wearing full oilskins with the sou'wester pulled down well over his eyes. He thought the man's face looked like nothing more than a big bushy beard.

"What do you want? How did you get in the locked door? Where did you come from?" asked Westerval.

"The way I came is the same way I'll return. But this time all I want is a line for the stern of my boat," said a hollow-sounding voice from the corner. Then the man gnashed his teeth so fearfully that Westerval shivered.

And now he knew who this figure was. It was undoubtedly the same fellow who had pounded on the floor underneath his house, and the very man who had robbed him of his night's sleep for so many long years.

A defiant stubbornness came over Westerval. The old, white-haired shopkeeper jumped over the counter and dashed straight for the fellow. With both fists he seized hold of the man's shaggy beard and shouted: "I tell you, in the name of God and all that is sacred, I'm not afraid of death! Back down to the sea bottom you go, you cursed corpse-eater!"

Two phosphorescent green eyes glittered from under the sou'wester. The stranger rammed his back against the door so the wood shredded like a rag. He turned and lurched among all the barrels and crates until he reached the floor hatch, which he yanked up and flung toward the ceiling. Then he dropped down into the sea.

"You may speak boldly on shore, Westerval. But you'll still be coming with me the third time," yelled the scornful voice from below.

Then came that memorable day when the hurricane tore down the church so that bits and pieces flew across the graves. That's when the fishermen had to sail for their lives out at sea. The storm had come upon them as if suddenly released from a sack.

Those on board one of the boats watched as another boat spun around. A few fishermen surfaced to clamber onto the overturned hull. They jabbed their knives into the wood and screamed with terror. Then huge, roaring sea swells swept them away. One man saw his brother die right before his eyes. Another man saw the same happen to his father. Yet it was impossible to offer any help.

Far off in the distance a boat both slender and fine raced through the sea so fast that foam sprayed all around it. That was Kristian Westerval, making his third trip as skipper. He sat at the tiller, his face pale but displaying a wildly defiant expression. He was going to show that corpse-eater that he was not afraid.

Old Jens Glea sat right next to Westerval, and later he told the story. Suddenly Johan Persa, who was sitting in the bow, shouted, "Dear Lord Jesus, I can see Ola and Lars lying on the hull over there!"

Then Westerval yelled, his face as white as chalk, "Grab them! We're going to run right over them!"

And over the capsized boat they flew, with a great scraping and grinding against the keel. Fists reached out on both sides. They got a good grip on Lars and hauled him up. But Ola was too heavy. He clung desperately to the gunwale, screaming horribly. The boat flew with such speed that phosphorescence sprayed around Ola, and the sea rose up, foaming white.

"Take the tiller, Jens!" bellowed Westerval. He leaned over the rail and reached down into the water to grab Ola, using immense effort as he tried to pull him up. Ola clutched at Westerval with all the strength of desperation.

At that moment a huge fist shot out of the water to grab Ola and pull him back down. Then another fist appeared and seized Westerval by the shoulder. He too was dragged down.

Holding on to the tiller, Old Jens watched with horror as those three in the water wrestled with each other in a violent battle. All of a sudden one of the figures grew into a gigantic fellow wearing oilskins. He grabbed Westerval by the throat and . . . That was the end. Then all three sank, and the boat raced away as swift as an arrow.

Everyone understood that it was the draug who had taken Westerval.

"He was a nice man," Old Jens said of Westerval. "Our Lord has opened the door of mercy to worse sinners than he ever was."

THE SEA SERPENT

About the sea serpent I can only surmise,
For I've not seen him with my own eyes,
Nor would I seek such an honor;
Yet those who've described him are not few
(Their words I find to be trusted and true!)
And he must be quite a horror.

—Petter Dass

There have always been quarrels and disputes about the sea serpent. Some folks will laugh in your face if you happen to mention it. Others will staunchly claim that the serpent does, in fact, exist. Even if they haven't seen it themselves, they might refer to an honorable grandfather or some other old person whose word they "find to be trusted and true."

Old Skipper Larsen—as honest an old salt as ever walked in a pair of sea boots—still insists today: "You can believe whatever you like, my man! But damn it, I've seen him! Yes, I have."

It's easiest for me to picture the sea serpent up north, where the vast, bare surroundings allow the eye and the mind a wild freedom. He must be gigantic. I'd like to see his head resting, with his mouth agape, near the island of Røst, on the outermost edges of the Lofoten archipelago, while he wraps his tail, one coil after another, around Træna, the rocky island far away. That place is compatible with the sea serpent's nature—the eternal foggy dreariness of the region, a desolate grayness as far as the eye can see.

Go ahead, landlubber, and steer in that direction in your little Nordland boat! The waves rise and fall with such gloomy monotony. The sea will grab you, overpower you—and you'll feel like a bit of dust floating on its deep, heavy breaths. Your mind will be caught in an iron ring. The vast and powerful sea will play with you. You're nothing but a speck that it doesn't even notice on its mighty, rolling back.

That's when you'll sense the monster lying below on the bottom, the horror of the sea! At any moment you'll see him rise, slimy and kelp-covered, slithering along with huge wriggling movements.

According to legend, the sea serpent was born on land. In a mound of rocks lies a tiny little serpent, squirming and wiggling about with malicious desires. His body is made up of multiple segments and looks as ugly as the tree larvae that crawl into the crown and strip away the leaves. As little as the serpent is, he's so vicious that he strikes and snaps at anything alive, with venom oozing out of his mouth. But when the serpent gets bigger and the space becomes too small, he has to make his way out. Then he creeps about in forest and field, from one mountain tarn to another, as he grows ever bigger and more vile—much to the dread and disgust of all living creatures. And nowhere can the serpent find any peace, for every place is too small for him. From one lake to another he plunges without ceasing, his eyes a glittering green. He wriggles and gnaws on his own flesh, propelled by his cursed life.

Then the serpent catches sight of the sea.

And the vast, mighty sea lures the serpent with its droning, melancholy song: "Sink, sink!" Down in the deep there is plenty of room, and beneath the raging storm there is calm for the eerie daylight, for the sharp, bright sounds that pierce like thorns.

Far below, at the very bottom, lies the serpent, getting bigger and bigger, miles long, endless, among the seaweed and sea slime, with thousands of plants and animals leeching onto his body.

Have you heard the lulling, muted tones from down there? Have you seen the horror of the sea bottom?

He wants to rise. Surfacing in all his vileness, lashing the sea into foam, then rolling with mighty sea swells, crushing Nordland boats and fishing vessels, terrifying people and animals. And laying waste to the sea.

Lord save us from the sea serpent!

Go ahead and sit out there in your Nordland boat on a gray and cold foggy day! The desolation and loneliness will wrap their straitjacket around you; they'll teach you to count every grain of sand sliding down in the hourglass of your life. Then the monster will come, chasing across the rolling sea swells, the horror of the sea bottom, that ghastly sea serpent!

THE TROLL BIRD

Far out at sea are several lonely and wild islands—jagged mountaintops that stick up in the most peculiar shapes, with swarming throngs of birds. Millions of rushing and flapping wings cause a teeming commotion in the air, above the sea, and on the mountaintops. You will glimpse all around nothing but the mighty blue sea. It rolls with great, wild swells and crashes among the skerries and cliffs with snow-white foam.

A dozen miles away lived a poor fisherman named Tosten. He often went to that area to fish, and then he would notice that things were not always as they should be out there on the bird island. He didn't dare go ashore. Something seemed to whisper to him that

it would not be wise to do so. But with each passing day he grew more and more curious, and he could find no peace. He thought the birds were staring at him with such strange-looking eyes whenever they flew over his head. And if they popped to the surface from under the sea, they always had something peculiar in their beaks. Once a puffin came flapping past with something that looked like two herrings hanging from either side of its beak. But the bird didn't seem to be seeing very clearly that day because it flew straight into the mast of Tosten's boat. And in its confusion the bird dropped the herrings into the boat. Tosten thought he heard a clinking sound, and when he looked closer he saw lying on the floorboards two big pieces of silver. "Aha!" Tosten said to himself.

One day he was fishing when such a vile storm blew in that he had to steer for his life as he desperately worked the sail. He raced past the bird island. The sea crashed and thundered in wild sheets all along the steep, dark mountainsides. Nowhere would it be wise to go ashore. Then Tosten happened to recall an islet farther away that was flatter. Maybe there he could seek shelter from the heavy swells.

His boat was carried from one breaker to another, each more powerful than the last. Sea spray lashed at his face with stinging ferocity, and every seam of the boat shook and shuddered. But Tosten stalwartly remained seated and held on to the tiller. All of a sudden a big black bird flew over his head. It cast a wild glance at him, then opened its dirty-yellow beak and spat into the boat. Tosten no doubt found that disgusting, but all that mattered was tending to the sail and oars. He was nearing the place where he planned to go ashore. Then he suddenly saw a towering, deep ebb tide with churning whirlpools of foam.

Tosten was a small and vigorous man. Swiftly he tore off his oilskins and sea boots, took down the sail, and sprang up onto the thwart, ready to jump.

The boat was carried toward shore on the back of a foaming wave, and just as it was about to crash, Tosten leaped in his stocking feet up the slippery mountainside with the sea thundering around him. Behind him the boat shattered, and the ebb tide dragged it away in bits and pieces.

Tosten's life was saved, but otherwise his prospects certainly weren't good. How on earth was he ever going to escape from this islet? Not a soul turned up in these parts for years on end. No doubt he'd be able to find shellfish and sea urchins to keep himself alive, but in the long run that would not be an especially pleasant diet. It was so desolate and dreary out here. Exhausted, wet, and miserable, Tosten wandered about as he looked for a place to spend the night. Among the sand dunes he found a hollowed-out space underneath several huge boulders, and he crept inside.

He hadn't been asleep long when he was awakened by a great screeching and commotion. Outside on the slope sat a crowd of coal-black birds. Several more came plummeting down to join the flock.

Then all of them cast aside their bird plumage, and there sat a group of strange little blue-clad fellows. They were clearly arguing about something. They ranted and raved at the top of their lungs, all of them yelling at once. But Tosten couldn't understand what they were saying. They seemed to be aiming most of their anger at a little gray-bearded figure sitting among them. They shoved and kicked him, and finally they grabbed hold of his beard and gave it a yank. After that they roamed about the islet, howling and shouting. At long last they put on their bird plumage again and, in one long line, flew over to the bird island.

Tosten lay there a long time, listening, before he dared venture out. The storm had subsided a bit, and there wasn't a living soul in sight.

Down on the foreshore he found the bailing bucket from his boat. Just as he was about to pick it up, he caught sight of that odd little gray figure. He was sitting on a rock and eating sea urchins—innards, spines, and all.

Tosten plucked up his courage and went over to him. But no sooner did the gray-beard notice the fisherman than he jumped to his feet and began gnashing his teeth, shrieking and carrying on so wildly that it was quite loathsome to behold. Tosten was so frightened that he threw the bailing bucket right at the fellow's forehead, causing him to topple over.

Next to him lay his bird plumage. That made Tosten very happy because he now had a free ride home. And he thought it only reasonable that this time he should take a closer look at what they were doing over on the bird island. He put on the plumage and flew off.

Over there, on the other side of the island, lay a big shipwreck. All around it swarmed tiny blue-clad men who were carrying casks and rolling barrels, busily pulling and dragging all manner of things. A bright blue light shone from a big door that stood open in the mountain, and inside Tosten could hear the jutul, the giant mountain troll, shouting and issuing orders.

Then Tosten knew what sort of folks they were. He turned around at once and headed for home as fast as he could go.

Back home people seemed to think that he was acting a bit odd. It was also strange that he had returned without his boat. Tosten said very little about his expedition, nor did he mention the bird plumage. He hid it safely in a pile of rocks. Occasionally he would take out the plumage and, if he had a chance, he would put it on and fly around a bit just for fun.

After a while he felt an urgent desire to go back to the bird island. So one day he put on the plumage and flew off. He didn't think those folks out there would be able to recognize him very easily.

Out on the island everything was the same, with lots of commotion and noise. With much flapping, Tosten landed in the middle of a flock of birds with the same plumage as his.

But that was a stupid thing to do. All the birds began babbling and talking at once. "Who's that?" "Who's that?" "Is that Sakarias?" "Is that you, Johan?" "Who can that be?"

Oh, thought Tosten, this is not a good place for me. I'd better sneak away. "It's me," he said then. And with that he lifted his wings and flew off as fast as he could go.

But then there was a huge ruckus. "It's Tosten!" "Grab him! It's Tosten!" In an instant the birds were after him, with a great rushing and rustling.

That was Tosten's last journey. Out on an islet they caught him and plucked him until he was as small as a kernel of grain.

A Jutul Battle

Up on the mountain plateau you're far above all things small. In the vast and solemn silence thoughts sail on outspread wings.

When the evening sun casts its glow from ridge to ridge, it's as if the great, hushed deity were wandering about and searching with a mighty lantern.

Like a lost little bird, I flutter about in the anxious silence of the stony wasteland. The slightest sound echoes as if inside a chasm. Everything towers with calm indifference around my trembling unrest. I feel the earth floating in the heavens; the racing clouds sweep across the back of my neck. Everything is so vast, everything is so desolate. Look, the sun is sinking! The blood surges in my veins, while in my heart a prayer quavers: "I refuse to let you go, Lord Jehovah, until you bless me!"

Overhead tumble dark storm clouds, and an icy wind speeds across the plateau, asking with a thousand tongues: "Where to? Where to?"

What sort of stalking commotion is shouting into the silence?

The clouds turn black. Then millions of raindrops rattle and drone all around, as if an immense and fearful pain has broken loose.

Crackling lightning shoots out from the black expanse of clouds. A violent thundering starts in the distance among the mountains.

No doubt that's not a goatherd ringing his bell this time!

But from inside the fog comes a shout that sends the scree rolling down the slopes. "I am the lord of Jotunheim!"

Two gigantic jutuls begin wrestling in a ferocious battle over the jagged mountaintops. The heights shudder, landslides thunder. Look over there! Blood is coursing like wild mountain streams, black and deep!

Now the sky opens its floodgates wide. Rain gushes and pours, thunder booms as if the planets in space were colliding, and lightning flashes, one bolt after another. Now Thor is throwing his hammer into Jotunheim! Take cover, take cover! Look, entire herds of reindeer are speeding this way, shattering rocks with their hooves. "Clip clop, clip clop. Take cover!"

It's suddenly as dark as the grave. Inside the mountains the angry giants growl. Thor's mighty hammer sends them into the shadows to hide.

The rain falls gently and quietly. Amid the solitude murmuring voices trickle from crevices and hollows and creek beds to report on the cacophonous event. In the silent darkness the voices gather into a humming song—the rustling of yellow leaves swirling from the tree of life.

But far, far away across the plateau an echoing rumble can still be heard: "I am the lord of Jotunheim. I want to be left alone. Do not intrude on my peace—or on the staring eyes of death!"

THE DYING MOUNTAIN TROLL

Inside the towering black peak there once lived a mountain troll who burst in the sun.

He lay inside the mountain, brooding in the dark over his heaps of gold and silver and gemstones. The treasures sparkled and glittered. Every time he looked at them, the gold would jingle and clink.

Then he happened to hear about the gold in the sky that was the sun. And he wanted to have it. Not in order to take delight in its rays—no, he simply wanted to have it, and then he would lock it away in his big copper chest.

One night he went out and began tearing at the scree to clear off the slopes. He toppled over big rocks and boulders as he bellowed and searched for the sun. Just imagine how it would gleam in his copper chest! The night was long and dark, and he was certain to find the sun. He tumbled and shoved the rocks, causing a thunderous noise, and live embers raced down the mountainside.

Far, far away among the ridges something seemed to be glowing. Not every little clod can shine in the dark, he thought. Maybe that's the sun.

Nope. It was nothing but a lousy little mountain lake!

He could see that he probably wasn't going about things the right way if he wanted to find the sun. It would be better to proceed more carefully.

But how should he do that?

He sat down at the top of Mount Raatanuten to ponder the matter.

Yet pondering isn't that easy either; it can be just as grueling as trying to find a sun. And a troll with twelve heads can have a hard time reaching an agreement with himself. There's never any peace when all the heads start talking at once. It leads to nothing but bickering and squabbling. Oh, yes, quite a lot of jabbering took place up there on Raatanuten! The heads spat and cleared their throats, they made faces at each other, and they banged foreheads whenever real fury overcame them. The only calm was possessed by the body on which the heads were attached. The quarreling went on all night long. Ugh, how vile that was! It sounded like someone whacking a tin bucket, like stones scraping on glass windowpanes, like the hum of spinning wheels, like deafening threshing machines, but also like snuffling noses and meowing cats—all pouring into the darkness!

Day is dawning. Light arrives, slowly rising. It offers warmth and delight, forgetting nothing. Sorrow and joy, jubilation and terror will all receive the same gentle kiss. The rays of light hold no hatred.

Now the first glow emerges above the dark mountain crests!

The bickering tongues fell silent. Horrified, the fearful creature rose and set off in a wild flight across peaks and pinnacles. Run! Run and hide among the gold and silver in the dark! He gnashed his teeth in futile rage and bit his own evil tongues, making blood gush. His clawed fingers clenched, his muscles and sinews grew as taut as tensed steel bows.

Then the sun appeared. He fainted, stumbled, collapsed. At the same time the poor mountain flower over in the cleft lifted its chalice to the day, filled with a shiny, silvery-clear dewdrop.

Far below in the valley, where small windowpanes glint, poor folks live who have little to eat or burn. The winter is so harsh and long. Much too long for such poverty. Nothing but snow and biting wind, snow and biting wind. And up on the towering heights are frozen, mocking faces. In the night and the dark they wander about in people's dreams, frightening and menacing!

Theodor Kittelsen, *Self-Portrait*, 1891. Oil on canvas, 60 x 45.5 cm.
National Museum for Art, Architecture, and Design, Oslo, Norway.
Photograph by Morten Thorkildsen.

CHRONOLOGY OF THE LIFE OF
THEODOR KITTELSEN

1857   Theodor Severin Kittelsen is born to Johannes Kittelsen and Guriane Olsdatter Larsen on April 27 in the coastal town of Kragerø in Telemark, Norway.

1868   To support his family after the death of his father, Kittelsen leaves school and becomes an apprentice to a watchmaker in Kragerø and then in Arendal, Norway.

1870   In Arendal, art historian Diderik Maria Aall sees Kittelsen's drawings and arranges to support his artistic education in the Norwegian capital, Kristiania (now Oslo). Aall's son Hans would later found the Norsk Folkemuseum.

1874   Kittelsen travels to Kristiania again to begin formal training as an artist. Architect Wilhelm von Hanno and sculptor Julius Middelthun are his mentors at the State School of Art.

1876–80   Kittelsen studies art in Munich for four years. Other Norwegian artists there at this time are Erik Werenskiold, Gerhard Munthe, Eilif Petersson, Christian Krohg, and Christian Skredsvig. Kittelsen begins contemplating a series of illustrations for Henrik Ibsen's *Peer Gynt*.

1879   Diderik Maria Aall informs Kittelsen that he is no longer able to financially sponsor the young artist's career. Kittelsen supports himself by selling drawings to German newspapers and magazines.

1880   Kittelsen receives a small scholarship that allows him to return to Norway.

1882   Kittelsen and Werenskiold, living near Kragerø, produce the first illustrations for a new collection of Norwegian folktales compiled by Peter Christen Asbjørnsen and Jørgen Moe. Kittelsen spends eight months painting in Paris.

1883   Kittelsen returns to Munich. Asbjørnsen and Moe's *Eventyrbog for Børn. Norske Folkeeventyr* is published and includes twelve drawings by Kittelsen, including "Ash Lad, Who Competed with the Troll."

1884   The second volume of *Norske Folkeeventyr*, featuring ten illustrations by Kittelsen, is published in Norway. A third volume in 1887 includes twelve of Kittelsen's drawings.

1886–87   Kittelsen and Werenskiold are asked by folklorist Moltke Moe to contribute illustrations to a Norwegian edition of Gabriel Djurklou's Swedish folktales for publisher Jacob Dybwad. Kittelsen produces nineteen drawings for the book and three watercolors for the cover.

1887–88   Frustrated by his poverty and longing for his homeland, Kittelsen leaves Munich and returns to Norway. He spends two years with his sister and brother-in-law tending the lighthouse at Skomvær, a rocky island in the Lofoten archipelago. Several of the drawings he produced here were published in *Troldskab* (Troll Magic) in 1892. Kittelsen continues to work on drawings for an illustrated edition of *Peer Gynt* in 1888. He completed his large oil painting *Ekko* (Echo), which was exhibited at the 1889 World Expo in Paris.

1889   In April, Kittelsen travels south and lives in a small cottage on Gopledahl, near Lake Farrisvann. He marries Inga Kristine Dahl in August. During their twenty-five-year marriage, they had eight children and adopted a ninth child.

1889–90	Kittelsen publishes the two-volume *Fra Livet i de smaa Forholde* (*Life in Narrow Circumstances*), a collection of drawings he created while living at Skomvær in Lofoten.
1890–91	Kittelsen purchases a small house at Hvisten on the Oslo fjord, where his family lives for five years.
1892–94	Kittelsen's years at Hvisten are highly productive, and he completes a series of illustrated social satires and fables. The collected illustrations are published in 1892 as *Glemmebogen* (*The Book of Oblivion*) and in 1894 as *Kludesamleren* (*The Rag-Picker*). His illustrations for *Troldskab* are published in 1892; Kittelsen had originally planned for these illustrations to be accompanied by writing by Norwegian author Jonas Lie, but when Lie's text never arrived, Kittelsen wrote the book himself.
1893	Kittelsen becomes consumed with the scenery and landscapes of southern Norway and embarks on a series of twelve colored-pencil drawings depicting areas around the rocky island of Jomfruland near Kragerø. The pictures in the Jomfruland series are accompanied by verses from "Description of Jomfruland," a poem written in 1696 by Kragerø's mayor, Roland Knudsøn. Though Kittelsen began a design for the collection, the illustrations were never published. He presents his first solo exhibition in October at Tivoli, a popular entertainment district in Kristiania.
1893–94	Kittelsen writes to Eilif Peterssen in December 1893 to report that he has just completed twenty-two humorous drawings in watercolor for Danish publisher Ernst Bojesen. *Har dyrene Sjæl?* (*Do Animals Have Souls?*) was published the following year and depicts animals with humanlike qualities, including toads, grasshoppers, snails, mice, and rats.

1894   While living at Hvisten, Kittelsen begins one of the most ambitious projects of his career, a series of illustrations depicting the Black Death that would eventually be published as *Svartedauen* (The Black Death).

1896   Having long desired a change in scenery to the mountains, Kittelsen sells the house at Hvisten and moves with his family to Sole near Eggedal, where they remain until 1899. He completes the last drawings for *Svartedauen* but struggles to find a publisher for the project. While living at Sole, Kittelsen is commissioned along with Norwegian artist Gerhard Munthe and several others to contribute decorations to the interior of the recently completed Holmenkollen Tourist Hotel near Kristiania.

1899   Kittelsen and his family build a house at Lauvlia in Sigdal and remain there for eleven years. The scenery around Lauvlia inspires some of Kittelsen's best-known landscapes.

1900   *Svartedauen* is finally published by J. M. Stenersen. The collection, designed personally by Kittelsen, includes forty-five drawings along with fifteen poetic texts. The National Gallery in Kristiania acquires twelve of Kittelsen's folktale paintings for its permanent collection.

1905   The Norwegian publisher Gyldendal commissions Kittelsen to create new illustrations for another edition of Asbjørnsen and Moe's *Eventyrbog for Børn. Norske Folkeeventyr*. The folktales and their illustrations had by this time become firmly established in Norwegian culture. Kittelsen also contributes to folktale collections by Hallvard Bergh and the unpublished tales by Reidar Müller.

1907–8   After visiting Rjukan and Notodden in 1907, Kittelsen begins five large fairy tale watercolors depicting the Rjukanfossen for Sam Eyde, director of Norsk Hydro. In 1908, Kittelsen is made a Knight of the Royal Norwegian Order of St. Olav.

1909–11   With his health failing, Kittelsen is forced to leave Lauvlia in the summer of 1909. Two years later he receives a grant from the Norwegian Parliament for his artistic achievements and publishes his autobiography, Folk og trold. Minder og drømme (People and trolls: Memories and dreams). He writes a retelling of the folktale "Soria Moria Castle" that features twelve of his paintings.

1912–14   In April 1912, Kittelsen purchases a property on the island of Jeløya near Moss, south of Oslo. He publishes a collection of miscellaneous drawings, Løgn og forbandet digt (Lies and cursed poetry). His final large-scale work, Peer Gynt i Dovregubbens hall (Peer Gynt in the Hall of the Mountain King), was completed in 1913.

1914   Kittelsen dies at Jeløya on January 21. His artistic career was celebrated with an exhibit later that year at the National Jubilee Exhibition at Frogner Manor in Kristiania.

—Compiled by Kristian Tvedten

THEODOR KITTELSEN (1857–1914) is one of Norway's most famous and popular artists, best known for his illustrations of Norwegian folklore. He illustrated *Eventyrbog for Børn. Norske Folkeeventyr*, a collection of Norwegian folktales compiled by Peter Christen Asbjørnsen, and by the early twentieth century his illustrations of trolls were well established in Norwegian culture. In 1887 he lived on Skomvær, a remote, rocky island in the Lofoten archipelago in northern Norway where he created many of the drawings in *Troldskab* (Troll Magic), which was published in Norway in 1892. He was made a Knight of the Royal Norwegian Order of St. Olav in 1908 for his artistic contributions, and his autobiography *Folk og trold. Minder og drømme* (People and trolls: Memories and dreams) was published in 1911.

TIINA NUNNALLY is an award-winning translator of Norwegian, Danish, and Swedish literature. Her many translations include *The Complete and Original Norwegian Folktales of Asbjørnsen and Moe* (Minnesota, 2019), as well as several books by Sigrid Undset. She was appointed Knight of the Royal Norwegian Order of Merit for her efforts on behalf of Norwegian literature abroad.

The University of Minnesota Press dedicates this book to
Linden Bennet Emmel Tvedten, fierce reader and avid troll hunter.

This translation has been published with the financial support of NORLA.

Originally published in Norwegian as *Troldskab* (Kristiania: H. Aschehoug, 1892).

The translator is grateful to Norsk biografisk leksikon and Norsk Kunstnerleksikon for their comprehensive biographical information on Theodor Kittelsen, and to Sverre Følstad, curator of the Kittelsen Museum in Blaafarveværket, Norway.

Frontispiece: Theodor Kittelsen, Skogtroll (Forest Troll), 1906. Pencil, watercolor, and gouache on paper, 36 x 28 cm. National Museum for Art, Architecture, and Design, Oslo, Norway. Photograph by Jacques Lathion.

Page iv: Theodor Kittelsen, Nøkken (The Water Sprite), 1904. Pen, watercolor, pencil, and crayon on paper, 47.5 x 69.4 cm. National Museum for Art, Architecture, and Design, Oslo, Norway. Photograph by Børre Høstland / Jacques Lathion.

Page 92: Theodor Kittelsen, Det rusler og tusler rasler og tasler (Creepy, Crawly, Rustling, Bustling), 1902. Pencil and watercolor on paper, 44 x 58 cm. Photograph copyright O. Væring Eftf. AS, Norway.

Translation copyright 2022 by Tiina Nunnally

Published by the University of Minnesota Press
111 Third Avenue South, Suite 290
Minneapolis, MN 55401-2520
http://www.upress.umn.edu

ISBN 978-1-5179-1139-3 (hc)

A Cataloging-in-Publication record for this book is available from the Library of Congress.

Printed in Canada on acid-free paper

The University of Minnesota is an equal-opportunity educator and employer.

30 29 28 27 26 25 24 23 22   10 9 8 7 6 5 4 3 2 1